WINTER

FREITS

Winter Freits

by

Andrew David Barker

Black Shuck Books
www.BlackShuckBooks.co.uk

First published in the UK by Black Shuck Books, 2019

978-1-913038-00-7

For Ben

Polar Vortex

I was born to constellations and blood. My skin felt alien to me; a frozen slab of meat harbouring a soul. There was a cut on my head. It felt deep. I felt open. There was blood in my right ear. I couldn't hear too well, could barely see. What I could make out was the universe glittering above me and my own ragged breath in the stillness. I did not know how long I'd been unconscious for.

With great effort I lifted my right arm and looked at my hand. In time my eyes focused, but I couldn't feel the hand. It looked almost translucent, ballooned and a bluey white. I dropped it back down. I was compacted in snow, deep snow. Everything glistened with frost. I saw a shooting star cut across the night sky and spark out and I wished on it.

I wished I knew who I was, then I passed out.

When I came round again I didn't know if only moments had passed or several hours; I had no sense of time. It was still dark though, the sky now alive with the silken emerald of the Aurora.

Beneath my many layers of clothing, every joint and limb of the body I inhabited felt frozen solid. Even the pain from the deep gash in my head – brilliant and all-encompassing before – now felt petrified and foreign. I was close to death, that much I knew. If I hadn't come round when I did I expect I would have just drifted away into the black. And truth be told, at that moment it did cross my mind to just sink back into unconsciousness, but I guess the instinct to survive doesn't let go that easily.

Plus, I could not die without knowing who I was. I had to move.

Through a force of will I didn't think myself capable of, I sat bolt upright. Ice crunched and cracked on my person, sounding very loud to even my muted ears. I sounded as if I were made of glass. My head fogged and I thought I was going to pass out again, but I held on, willing myself to stay in the world. And what world was this? A white world – it looked so strange with the Aurora blazing its ribbons of green across the night, and its luminous shadows dancing over vast, endless snow dunes; a world so still and silent I doubted for a moment whether it was even real or not. I *chose* to believe it was real, however, because the alternative would suggest that I was, in fact, already dead.

But *where* was I? Was I looking up at the Aurora Borealis or Australis? I tried to pick out constellations, but the green sky was so rich with stars, and my head so fogbound, I had difficulty focusing. Instead, I looked about me. A black ridge of hills lay beyond the vast expanse of white, while to the other side of me, a lake glistened green, a glass mirror to the sky. I shifted round on my behind and saw the dark blood on the snow where my head had been. Beyond that lay a rucksack, frosted over, and further still I saw something that quite startled me. A cabin.

I turned over onto all fours, and tried to push myself up, but it was futile. There was simply no strength in me; I couldn't even get my knees to leave the ground. My breath plumed out before me and colours dotted my vision. I almost crumpled headfirst into the snow, but I somehow managed to regain control by closing my eyes and focusing on my breathing – long, slow intakes of bitterly cold air. I blinked the colours from my eyes and slowly lifted my head, trying to locate the cabin door. It stood about fifteen yards away. I was going to have to drag myself to it.

It was slow, painful work. Just to the right of the blood, my hand found a sharp rock hidden beneath the snow. I must have slipped over and smashed my head against it, spilling out my memories along with blood.

I didn't allow myself to dwell on this, however. I pressed on, quickly becoming short of breath once again. The dots returned to my eyes and I had to stop. I raised my head, blinked at the colours in my vision, and looked at the cabin door. It looked so close and so impossibly far. I continued on, dragging my body through the snow.

I stopped twice more before I reached the door, the second time for many minutes, but each time I forced myself onwards. I had virtually no strength and the pain in my head was so immense I wondered how I could possibly still be alive, let alone conscious. There was a sharp metallic taste in my mouth, and as I neared the door I threw up into the snow. There was blood in the vomit. It spoiled the pure white and looked grotesque. I gagged, but nothing more came out.

I reached the door at last, hoping to God it was unlocked. I looked back and saw the rucksack near the dark spill of blood. If the door was locked, and the keys were in the rucksack, then I was as good as dead. The thought of undertaking the journey I'd just done, not once but twice more, filled me with a dread beyond thought and reason. I felt so angry at myself for having left the rucksack. Angry and stupid. I'd been distracted by the rock I'd found in the snow – the rock which had cost me my memory – and the rucksack just hadn't seemed important at that moment.

I reached up and tried to grab the door handle, the tips of my fingers just touching it. My arm fell back down. I thought then that I was going to die right there on the stoop of that cabin. I was so exhausted; having to reach for the handle a second time seemed quite impossible. But try I did, this time using the door to pull myself up onto my knees. I gripped the handle. It was made of wood, crafted into the door itself, and was bitterly cold – colder perhaps than even the snow. I yanked it down and suddenly the door opened inwards.

I fell into the cabin, hard.

Kicking the door shut with my foot, I tilted my head and tried to get a sense of the cabin. The first thing I noticed was the fire, glowing red with embers. A stack of wood lay in a companion on the hearth, along with a small tin bucket filled with kindling. I managed to crawl along the floor to the fireplace; it was made of brick and blackened with soot. I sat before it, shivering madly, and gently placed a few choice pieces of kindling into the grate until the fire caught again.

Once it was going strong, I piled wood on and warmed my fingers. I unzipped my jacket, sodden as it was, and cast it aside. I unlaced my boots and took them off, along with the several pairs of socks I was wearing, and warmed my toes before the fire. I examined my feet and saw they were red and blotchy, and I wondered if I had chilblains, or worse, frostbite.

The fire created dark and lively shadows about the cabin. There was a bed, a toilet and other amenities in the far corner, a kitchen to the back of the cabin, and by the front window, overlooking the frozen lake, a desk, which was overflowing with paper and open books. Nearer to me, an extremely worn and well-lived-in chair stood at the fireside. I touched it with the soles of my feet. There was also a settee in the centre of the room, accompanied by a table as cluttered as the desk, and beside the settee stood a darkened Christmas tree, its decorations threadbare and very crude. I figured I should try and get up and make it over to the sink and tend to my head, but I couldn't move. I didn't want to leave the fireside. So I lay there, the fire giving life back to my thawing body. And now I was (relatively) safe and warm, my mind turned to the myriad of questions I had been keeping at bay. The most prominent of which was *who am I?*

I realised that I didn't know what my voice sounded like. Of course, I'd grunted and moaned as I dragged myself to the cabin, but my speaking voice was a complete mystery to me. Somehow, at that moment, not knowing my own voice seemed stranger to me than not knowing my own mind. So I spoke.

"Who am I?"

The words sounded hollow, and barely registered above the crack and snap of the fire. My voice was croaky, and perhaps didn't truly represent my actual voice very much. Yet hearing it brought about a wave of emotion I was not expecting. It saddened me to hear my voice, so tiny and ragged, and I felt overwhelmed with my plight, and the fragile and pitiful thread by which my life hung. I had trouble understanding this rush of sorrow at first, and then I realised that hearing my own voice confirmed something to me – that I was actually real, that my mind *was* lost, and with that, sadness bloomed.

"Who am I?" I said again, now crying.

I looked down at my body. Firelight cast over me. It looked to be a middle-aged body, my breasts small, my stomach soft, my hips wide. I surmised that I was a woman of around forty, maybe a little older. I wondered if I'd had a child, and the not knowing brought on another wave of tears. I looked over to the sink in the toilet area, and to the mirror that hung above it. The desire to look upon my face overcame me and I struggled to my feet, using the tatty old chair to lever myself up. With great effort I finally stood.

My head fogged once more, but I closed my eyes, held onto the chair and waited out the haze. Managing to regain control, I began to take small steps across the cabin. My legs felt very shaky, but I took it slow and steady.

The floorboards creaked beneath me, and I realised that my hearing was becoming clearer. I took several stumbling steps across the room and came to the bed, using it to steady me, then I pretty much lunged at the sink. I gripped it hard and looked at my reflection.

A stranger looked back at me.

Her hair was short and dark and matted with blood; her features sharp, not entirely unattractive, but by no means beautiful. The eyes, on the other hand, *were* beautiful, however haggard they looked – big and green and glistening with life, which quite startled me. They were remarkable eyes and I stared at them, and they stared back at me, but absolutely no recognition came. It was a proud and predominant face; it held grace, and strength, and intelligence, yet it was stranger's face. The woman in the mirror was a complete mystery to me. An alien wearing my soul.

I closed my eyes and leaned over the sink, then I threw up. Again there was blood in the vomit – blood and whatever this woman last ate. Most of it was watery though and I had to gag and retch to get it all out. It hurt my throat and reignited the blinding pain in my head. When it was finally over, I slumped to the floor, one hand raised, still gripping the edge of the sink. I kept my eyes closed, trying to master the pain in my skull. The woman's skull.

I could neither think clearly nor find the will to move, the pain was just too intense. I imagined the pain as a wild and erratic firecracker shorting out all my wiring, scorching my mind until there was nothing left but an empty head, leaving this mindless entity to walk around attached to a body of age and experiences lost to the fire. I was the alien inhabiting an unknowable skin.

I, or she (I now had trouble thinking of myself as *I*), leaned back against the wall by the sink and looked out across the cabin. Through the window above the desk I could see the wavering green sky, and this, coupled with a cabin dressed in flickering red and black shadows, looked eerie, and quite beautiful. I tried to get my thoughts in order. The pain in my head had dissipated somewhat, enough for me to think a little clearer anyway, and I began to make a mental list of what I *did* know.

I was a woman of around forty, alone in a cabin in the far north of the world. I wondered how I knew this for sure, and could find no real answer; I just seemed to know it. However, why I was stationed in such an unforgiving land was unknown to me. It then struck me as funny that I knew about the Aurora – that vaporous majesty, caused by solar winds battering against the earth's magnetosphere – and knew nothing of my own self. It seemed like a particularly cruel joke. I then wondered what else I knew of the world (and the universe, for that matter). I knew of countries, and cities, continents and nations, and a little of stars and planets. I knew London, I realised. I could picture its labyrinthine streets, and the smog, and noise, and smell. I knew its smell! But the woman whose eyes had stared out from that mirror, so green and beautiful, was utterly remote.

I spoke out loud again, "Why am I here?", and confirmed to myself that I was indeed English.

I tried to guess as to what year it might be,

but this alluded me also. I thought perhaps the mid-eighteen hundreds. However, this just didn't feel right. For one thing, I could picture two Londons. One was lamp-lit and fogbound, all shadows and flame, the other, a city of light, with great towers mapping the skyline. I began to have a vague notion of great trains intersecting beneath the city, but this came to me like a half-remembered dream, hazy and fragmented.

I felt exhausted and closed my eyes, trying to empty my already empty head of any further questions. Then, summoning the strength from somewhere, I busied myself with the mundane. I stood once more and washed the blood from my hair (and ear) as best I could. I was surprised when I turned the tap and water came out. It was a little murky, but still, I thought this a miracle. It was even hot, which I found more astonishing, and soaking my hair (and wound) felt wonderful, if quite tender. Beside the toilet, which I used after I washed my head, was a bath, and now knowing I had hot water, I began to fill it. As the water ran, I shuffled around the bed and came to a wardrobe. The woman's clothes hung like ghosts. I stood looking at them for a long time. Finally I moved. I laid out trousers, a vest and a thick woolly jumper on the bed, then returned to the bath. I tested the temperature, added a little cold water, and then stepped in.

The woman's joints ached terribly, and the ends of fingers and toes tingled sharply, and most unpleasantly. The bath was so positioned that I could still look across the cabin to the window above the desk, and to the majestic sky beyond. The fire popped and hissed as it ate away the logs and continued to dance its merry red jig about the cabin walls. From that white world outside the door, there was not a sound.

I slipped my head under the water. It stung the wound, but I remained beneath the surface for as long as my breath would hold. When I rose up, there was a figure stood by the fireside.

It was a face, followed by shadow, rather than an actual solidified being. The face was a man's, bearded and dirty, with dark, terrible eyes that glinted in the fire glow. They stared at me with horrific intensity. Then it shifted like shadow – the whole being that is, the head along with the shape that carried it. The features stretched and bent around the creases and angles of the cabin's interior. It appeared to merge into other shadows cast by the fire, until the face was gone and the entire presence became but a black shape going about the walls. I watched this nebulous move across the ceiling until it was eaten by fire shadows.

The entire encounter lasted mere seconds, but the afterimage of that terrible face lasted far longer. The thing that horrified me above all, however, was that my own face had been nothing but a stranger to me, but the man's face had brought about an awful recognition.

I got out of the bath, towelled myself down and began to dress. It felt good to finally have dry, warm clothes on me. I walked over to the fire, stoked it, added more wood, then gathered up the pile of sodden and steaming clothes and carried them over to the kitchen area. I threw them in a corner – I felt too tired to deal with domestic chores just at that moment. I found several bottles of alcohol on the kitchen worktop. There was whiskey, brandy, and vodka. I choose the brandy, finding a glass in a cabinet fixed to the wall. I poured a very healthy measure and returned to the fireside.

I sat in the tatty old chair – which I sank into

– and sipped at the brandy and gazed into the fire. I wondered how I could be so composed. My hands remained steady, as did my heart. Yet I'd awoken, frozen and near-death with no knowledge of my own self. The woman whose body I inhabited, was a complete stranger to me; as was the cabin in which she lived. I was cut off in a remote and unforgiving land – I dreaded to think how far from the nearest pocket of civilisation I was – and quite why and how this woman came to live in such a place was positively unfathomable. And then there was the face that had visited me: An unwanted spectre of ghastly malevolence that, quite terribly, somehow meant more to me than any of this. And still, my hands and my heart remained steady.

Perhaps it was because I felt so detached? Although I could feel this woman's body, and the pain it had so bitterly endured, it felt remote somehow. It was as if it were happening to someone else, only I could feel their torment through several degrees of separation. An extreme synaesthesia. Even the foul visitation was looked upon as if through someone else's eyes, and therefore my fear had remained in check, if not exactly dormant. Perhaps *I* was the ghost?

This thought came suddenly and brought about a revulsion so all-consuming I thought I may pass out again. I swallowed down the remainder of the brandy and then threw the glass into the fire, where it smashed, loudly. I stood and begin to pace, my shadow bending and elongating about the walls and ceiling, not unlike the spectre's. Is this what it means to be a ghost, I thought: to haunt an unknowable soul and, in turn, to be haunted yourself? Did I lose, not only my mind out there in the snow, but also my life? Perhaps this place was a kind of purgatory?

Of course, not one of these hazy questions could I answer. I walked over to the window, leaned on the desk, and looked out across to the frozen lake beyond. It still shimmered green beneath the sky fire of the Aurora. There was also a shape moving upon it.

It shifted and stretched; in no way imprisoned by gravity, or any such law of nature that I knew of. It morphed, moving across the ice, at one moment black and shapeless, the next shimmering white, forming into the outline of a being. Whenever it did this, the figure was slender and, I thought, feminine, but its form never fixed for more than a second before it shifted its texture and shape once again, so any clear determination of sex was futile. What I did know in an instant, however, was that it was not the spectre from before. Even from far off across the frozen lake, I could tell (*feel?*) there was no such malevolence in this scrag.

I watched it reach the edge of the lake, then displace and roll out like a dying fogbank. The Aurora had also dimmed, only lightly painting the sea of stars now. The sky was dawning in the east, over the dark shoulder of hills. The spectre was gone.

I sat down at the desk, the chair creaking beneath me. Before me was a large stack of pages, all hand-written in a messy, almost illegible scrawl, and about the desk were notes scribbled on torn bits of paper; open-flat books, their spines cracked and well-worn; a drawing of a ramshackle rookery by night; teetering and cramped houses, wretched hovels all, with broken windows patched with rags and paper, and narrow and gloomy streets festering with vermin, both rat and human – I felt I *knew* this place.

To the back of the desk sat a picture frame. In it was myself (or the woman whose body I was haunting) and a man. It looked to have been taken in a park during autumn time; they stood embraced on a path scattered with fallen leaves and lined with red and gold trees. If this woman – who had longer hair and a little more weight – was indeed me, then this autumn sojourn was utterly lost to my mind, as was the man. Handsome though he was, I recognised him not a jot. Nevertheless, they looked happy and very much in love, and without really understanding why, my eyes welled up with tears. It seemed like a particularly bad joke that I would get so emotional about a man – a lover, or husband perhaps – that I no longer knew at all; but, of course, that was the entire point. I had lost everything in a stupid fall out in the snow, and now my life, and the people that inhabited it, were gone to me.

And what of this man? Where was he? His presence was decidedly absent throughout the cabin in all but the picture; there were no clothes, no evidence whatsoever of anyone else being here but her. Yet he must have been very important to this woman's life to still take pride of place on her desk. But why was she here alone? Were they estranged? Was he simply in another part of the world? Or was he dead?

Bitterly, this seemed closer to any truth I could reach for. I felt a single tear run down my face. I wiped it away and tried to laugh off the tide of emotion that attempted to seize me. How could I cry for a man I could no longer remember, whose fate I did not know? I couldn't, I decided. I wouldn't allow it to get the better of me, and so I stood up and crossed the room to the fire. I stoked it once more, and added another log; it crackled as the flames embraced it. I felt utterly exhausted and thought perhaps I should try and get some sleep. I looked over to the bed. The woman had made it – the woman I once was, but no longer.

I walked across the cabin, pulled back the covers and got in still wearing my clothes. My fractured and fragile mind, and the overwrought body that housed it, slipped away almost immediately. My last thought before I drifted off was, *perhaps my dreams will tell me who I am.*

My dreams, however, were feverish; a kaleidoscopic nightmare that bled in a seemingly endless precession. There was a dirty river, on the banks of which children foraged in the mud, and fog wisped about them in shreds and tatters; I dreamt of a thronging rookery, a place honeycombed deep within a great city, where thieves, prostitutes, and magsmen jostled and sloshed against the filth, and rot, and garbage of the slum.

I also dreamt of the other great city; the one made of light and glass, the shimmering citadel of towers. I *knew* these places. I dreamt of the spectre on the frozen lake, and of the hideous face that moved about the cabin walls like a large spider. I dreamt of blood, and snow, and the vast cosmos ribboned with the emerald manifest of solar winds.

I dreamt of the woman in the mirror.

I woke with a start, sweaty and shivering. My mouth was dry and tasted foul. In the cold light of morning, the cabin looked quite different. For one, I noticed things I had not in the dark. There were Christmas presents beneath the tree, colourfully wrapped in seasonal paper; there was a pantry off the kitchen, its door ajar. It looked well stocked – which gave me much relief as I had awoken quite ravenous – and there were more pictures of myself (if *she* was really me) with either the man from before, or other people, strangers all.

I pulled back the covers and sat on the edge of the bed. The fire was down, nothing but ash now, glowing in parts. I could see my breath plume out before me. The large window beyond the desk had frosted over. There were strange markings seemingly scratched into the frost; lines, weird symbols, and even, and this made my stomach lurch, an eye.

I stood up and walked over to the desk, the floorboards creaking beneath me. The sun was hitting the glass and the frost was steadily melting away, but the scratch marks were still very predominant, and deeply unsettling. Someone (*something*) had clawed at my window as I slept. The spectre of the lake, perhaps, or the face; I pictured that dark and hungry visage peering in at me, and I shivered. I looked at the scratched-in eye and felt incredibly weary. I had to steady myself against the desk. I turned my back on the window, deciding that food was what I needed, and strode over to the pantry. As I moved, however, every hair on my neck prickled as I felt the scratcher scrag watch me from outside.

I went about the prosaic task of preparing some kind of breakfast. I simply went through the motions, my mind elsewhere the entire time. In the pantry I found stack of canned food; soups, chopped tomatoes, (quite unappetising) meats, pilchards; also bags of potatoes, various vegetables, oats, and large bottles of water. I also discovered an ice box which contained frozen meats, milk, bread, and so forth. I took milk and a loaf of bread from the freezer and placed them on the kitchen work surface to defrost, then I lit the stove (I found a drawer filled with matches, cookware, and other odds and ends), and busied myself preparing a bowl of porridge. The cabin had gas and water, but no electricity.

While the porridge was boiling, I went over to the Christmas tree and picked up one of the presents. The box felt light. I decided to open it, hoping whatever lay inside might give some clue as to who I was. I tore away the paper to reveal a cardboard box. I opened it and found it was empty. Puzzled, I opened another and again found an empty box. Then I opened another, and another, and another, until everything was open. There was not a gift to be found. These Christmas presents had been merely decorative.

I wondered about how lonely this woman must have been.

I returned to the porridge. I had made rather a lot, and helped myself to two bowls full.

I sat on the settee while I ate and watched clumps of ice run down the bay window. The markings, including the eye, steadily dissolved away, and by the time I'd finished eating and got the fire going again, the window was, by and large, clear. Sunlight streamed through in long shafts and I lay back on the settee watching dust particles, wondering what my next plan of action should be. I lay there for a long time before deciding that I'd better head outside and check my surroundings. It also occurred to me that I should retrieve my rucksack and go around the cabin and see if there was any more wood for the fire, as the logs on the hearth had depleted considerably.

I continued to lie there working out my plan.

After I'd checked outside, I would come back in (hopefully with more wood to see me through the night), make myself a more substantial meal, then sit and read everything that lay scattered about the woman's desk (*my* desk). That all settled in my mind, I decided to allow myself five more minutes rest.

When I finally woke up, the light was pale and blue. Night was coming on.

I'd been out all day.

I was furious with myself for having slept so long. I found myself pacing around the cabin, chuntering to my idiotic self for allowing the entire day to slip away like that. Then it occurred to me that daylight hours would be very short – five, maybe six hours at the most. But still, this realisation didn't quell my anger any. If anything, it made matters worse. The finite amount of daylight I had, I'd wasted. I had to act fast.

The fire was now out, with only a few scraps of wood left to rekindle it. Without more logs I was in for a bitterly cold night. Moreover, I was now starving, and the thought of facing another long night (without having seen hardly any daylight) was almost unbearable to think about. The hunger part I could address, but without a fire, in my weak state, I could be in serious trouble.

Also, another night with the chance of visitations from spectres filled me with an almost paralysing dread.

I decided to take a look outside, as I had planned to do several hours before, to see if I could find any more firewood in storage. If there wasn't any, I would have to find something – anything – that I could burn instead, and I had to do this quick before the sun went down.

I wasted no time. I put on my boots – which had dried out nicely – and my coat – which was still a little damp in places – and found fresh gloves and even a woolly hat on a coat-rack near the pantry. Then, with a deep breath, I stepped out into the white world.

In an eerie half-light, I stumbled out into snow. I latched the cabin door behind me and took a long sharp breath of freezing air. Remarkably, the cold felt even greater than the previous night. It burrowed into the very marrow of the woman's bones, and I knew that without fire, my chances of surviving the night would be very slim indeed.

The sky was a pale blue, deepening into night over the hills far off to the east. The first stars were born to this coming night in scatterings, and a ghost moon was on the rise. There was no Aurora.

I looked across the frozen land. In this gloaming, the icy lake seemingly bled into the whites of the snow. Without me knowing it was there, it would have been difficult to make out. It looked almost ghostly in and of itself; something that could only be half-glimpsed and doubted as a truth. Again I wondered if I was actually dead, and if this place was indeed my purgatory. The land and its tricks of light and distortion certainly felt supernatural. Perhaps, I thought, in death we are washed clean of our memories and become but empty souls left to wander barren worlds in search of answers that never come. A particularly cruel joke indeed.

First, I went to retrieve my rucksack. It was frozen solid, but it wasn't zipped up the whole way. I shoved my hand in and grabbed the first thing I found. My heart leaped when I realised what it was. A radio.

Joy and relief were short lived, however, when I discovered that it was completely frozen and completely dead. I cried out and threw the radio as far as I could. I immediately regretted this, but I didn't go and look for it. The main thing to find was firewood and I couldn't afford to waste what little energy I had looking for a broken radio.

The only other items in the rucksack were some food and a blanket. All frozen solid. This woman had clearly left in a hurry. I dropped the rucksack and returned to the cabin. There was still blood in the snow trailing up to the door.

I began to walk around the cabin. The snow was hard and compact under foot, and I lost my balance several times. I did not fall, however; somehow I managed to remain on my feet. I trudged along slowly, using the cabin to steady me. I came around the side and saw my first view of what lay behind the cabin: an expanse of white, and beyond that, a ridge that led up to a forest, the snowy tree line stretching as far as I could see. It looked dense and unforgiving, yet it also stirred in me a glimmer of hope; a hope that beyond it lay some kind of civilisation. Its unknowable size was a great concern, however.

I pushed on.

I went around the back of the cabin; still no sign of any firewood. I began to get gravely concerned.

I passed a small window that looked in on the bedroom and glanced inside. My legs nearly gave out beneath me. The black mass was shifting and elongating up the wall beside the bed, a hideous spectre of shape-shifting shadow. It seemed to sense my presence as it quickly scurried into a dark corner of the ceiling. It happened so fast that I doubted what I had seen almost instantly. I stood rigid, my breath – one of the few things that convinced me that I was indeed alive – heavy and ragged. I peered in once more, my heart pounding against the woman's chest, but *it* was gone; the only shadows that remained were the ones created by the sun's dying light.

I composed myself as best I could and moved on. The idea of having to go back inside the cabin filled me with utter despair. I thought of running to the forest and trying to get as far away from this dreadful place as I possibly could, but knew, of course, that would be certain death. Without provisions, some kind of shelter, and many more layers of clothing I probably wouldn't even make a mile, not in my weakened condition.

I came around the other side of the cabin and there I was greeted with the glorious vision of an outhouse and work shed. My spirits lifted. Truth be told, they positively soared. There were piles of wood, chopped and stacked, ready for burning. I could keep death at bay, at least for one more night.

I spent a considerable amount of time carrying wood inside the cabin. I could only manage one or two logs at a time, and the going was painfully slow. I brought in far more than a single night required, but wanted to get as much wood as I possibly could in case my strength failed me completely, or a snowdrift moved in, or any other numerous reasons why I might not be able to venture outside again over the days ahead. By the time I was satisfied I had enough inside, I was sweating profusely, felt utterly drained, and full dark had fallen.

I shut the cabin door and took off my coat and gloves. I lit candles about the cabin, then rekindled the fire and sat before it, stoking and adding timber. It was soon aflame once more and I drank in its heat.

After a spell before the fire, I went across to the bathroom and undressed. I didn't bathe, but washed my face and underarms in the sink. I then redressed in new clothes foraged from the woman's wardrobe and began to prepare a meal. I made soup on the gas stove and sliced up the loaf of bread I'd defrosted earlier, then I sat on the settee before the fire and ate the food. I was ravenous and helped myself to several helpings of the soup, and ate the entire loaf.

And so, with my belly full and the fire ablaze, I sat down at the desk overlooking the frozen lake and began to read the stack of pages upon it.

It looked to be a manuscript of some sort, but its order was scattered; no one page followed another. The writing was in long hand and very difficult to read. I made out one name that kept being mentioned – Ranskul – and something about it echoed in my brain, along with a place called Jacob's Island, but for the most part the manuscript was illegible. There was one line, however, that was so clear on the page, it was as if it had been written by an entirely different hand altogether.

Let those black hills tremble.

It made little sense to me, at least at first, but something about its lyrical and malevolent implication struck me. I looked to the dark shoulder of hills across the lake. In the strange light of this place, the seemingly endless dance of flickering reality, those black hills did appear to tremble. Perhaps, I thought, this place was an illusion; an elaborate conjuring trick. An echo chamber for a life, or perhaps many lives, once lived and lost. Perhaps this was nothing but a fever dream state. Perhaps I was lying on a hospital bed somewhere, hooked up to an array of blinking and beeping monitors, with my family around me, all fraught with worry, waiting for me to wake up. Or perhaps this place was nothing but my dead reckoning.

I wondered how long it would be before someone discovered me frozen solid. Would I ever be found?

As these, and many more, fluttering thoughts strangled up my mind, I found a piece of paper with these words written upon it:

Ajáito, Ajáito... the name meant nothing to me. I cried out in frustration. Then I saw a black mass moving down by the ice lake. It was not the spectre of light, but the black scrag that seeped malevolence and terror.

I watched it through the window. It was far off, but I could see it clearly, shifting across the white. It seemed to be almost a dance, some ritualistic masquerade, or a taunting of sorts. Above, the sky was ablaze with stars and their beauty was painful. I wondered about how vast the universe was, and how, in all that space, I ended up here, with whatever haunts this place. When I looked back to the black thing, it was gone.

I leaned back in the chair. It creaked. The wind whispered at the door, at the windows. I held my breath and listened. The night offered nothing.

Then my spine quivered as I realised that the black scrag was behind me.

I felt its presence at the nape of my neck. Felt it looking at me, probing me. I couldn't move. I looked at the words on the page in front of me.

I have to get the hell out of this place.

I had written that. Or the person I used to be had written that. Whoever I was, she knew that there was something very wrong with this place. I felt the slightest touch of a finger. It ran down the side of my neck, to my shoulder. The touch seemed to penetrate my mind, locking something into place. Memories all rushed toward me at once. A phantasmagoria of visions.

The black scrag gave me back not just my recent life, but the life I led before that. A hurricane of knowledge.

I rocked back and forth in the chair. Outside, the sky shot through with green, the black hills trembled, the icy lake gave its silky reversal of image. I felt my eyes roll up inside my head as the scrag – Ranskul, I was sure – ran his fingers through my hair. His long nails nicked at the scar on my scalp. Inside my head, the hurricane raged.

The rookery, Jacob's Island, the piss and shit of countless dregs, the shuffling hordes, fucking and fighting and crawling and tearing and gasping into a life lived in such a low place. The lowest place. My name was Susan, born into the dirt and left to fend for myself. A mudlark, a criminal, a whore.

I saw myself looking to the lights of the city. The place just beyond the water, but so far out of reach. London, the city of nets, the city of blood and money and power. We be the wretches, cast out from it heart, to live like animals in the twisting, turning shacks, piled upon one another. All of us hungry for one thing. Survival.

I am there again. I watch the smokestacks, hear the city beating. Its heart is black, but very strong. It chimes in my mind.

I feel Ranskul inside me. In my sex. Thrusting into me. I feel his sweat dripping on my back. I feel his fingers tear at my flesh, pull at my hair, grab at my neck. I feel him come into me, then I feel the knife slice at my neck, my breasts, my stomach. I open my eyes and see the mud on the ground, and the shit and smell the stink. There are others walking past me, but they do not stop Ranskul. Nobody stops Ranskul.

I hear my screams, I feel my fear. It has a metallic taste to it. Bitter and overwhelming. He makes slices in me at first. Little cuts. Deep enough to torture, but light enough to keep me alive.

Ranskul. The black shape. The scrag at my back. Was once a man. Mortal. He pissed and shat and ate and drank and killed his way through his short, horrendous life. He was the horror of Jacob's Island. There was no law there, no courts, no reckoning. He was his own judge, jury and executioner. A murderer, with a penchant for young women. Women of the streets, of the night. Women like Susan. The woman I once was.

He is bent over me. Long black hair, beard thick and wiry. Eyes like the night. I see my blood run into the mud. A foot steps in it and walks on.

He grows distant. Then London and the island and Ranskul and the night all fade from sight.

I came out of this fever dream for the briefest of moments. Long enough to see the world outside thick white, dense and swirling; a vortex of ferocious power. I heard it tearing at the cabin. Before I sunk back under I had enough time to think this thought:

I am being haunted by the man who killed me.

I was born to a new life. A different time, a different name, a different social status. Born to a city of glass, with electric roads of sleek and superfast vehicles, and neon, and an absence of human connection. I know this time as well as I knew the 19th century. Where my soul had been in the two hundred years between the two ages, I did not know. Drifting perhaps, waiting for a vessel, a harbour in skin.

I saw artificial beings, and towers eaten by clouds, and trains of impossible speeds, and the multitudes locked into their devices and me, now Judy, married, in a glass tower. London again, but a very different London. Now a megalopolis, a super city, a technological marvel. Yet shadows of the old city remained here and there, but they were fragments, like ghosts themselves. But London is, after all, a city of ghosts. They are legion. Everywhere you turn, even in its charged and modern architecture, there are still cracks in the pavement, and alleyways that lead back in time.

Judy was a writer. Judy, the woman whose face and body I possessed, was an author of fictions. Fictions set in the 19th century, in the low places, the rookeries, the black shanties. These fictions took people away from the megaworld, back to an age of smoke and fog and darkness.

Judy had always been drawn to that long-ago world, ever since childhood. She studied it, mastered its qualities, and poured it out onto the page. It made her money and made her name. But as much as that world entranced her, so too did it haunt her.

She lost a child in birth and became withdrawn. She fell into the arms of other men. She did not write. Her husband left her, and she drank. The megaworld felt alien to her. It always had.

Then, in her darkest hour, she decided to leave England, and head North, to the white lands, to turn her back on the world, and write, and reconnect with herself.

As for the name Ajáito, he was a local and knew these lands. He led Judy here, led *me* here, set me up, and returned each fortnight with fresh supplies. Her fictions had brought her fame and money, but now she was lost, and cut off from the world. This was meant to be the place she reconnected with the page, with her art, and with herself. But what she found out here was something else entirely.

What she found here was the black scrag.

It lingered, waiting for the soul it had once

desecrated. It haunted her, day and night, and delirium set in.

Finally, Judy ran out into the night, fell, cracked her head and bled her mind out onto the snow. And the women that were two parts of the same soul each grasped for memories. Susan and Judy, twins, forged over two hundred years apart. Both haunted by a most foul and blackest of scrags, a diabolical freit.

And so, in this sudden clarity of vision and place in life, I, Judy, Susan, raced from the cabin and out into the polar vortex.

White out. A world swallowed whole. The wind was piecing to the ears. The cold, burning to the skin. In just a few steps, the cabin became a faint etching within the swirls of white. Somewhere, deep within the labyrinth of tangled minds I now possessed, I knew without a shadow of a doubt that I would die out here within minutes, yet I could not go back into that cabin – that place where Ranskul, the black scrag, lay in wait for me.

I walked further out and soon the cabin was gone from sight. Nothing but white, raging, turning, howling all about me. I stood, closed my eyes, waited for the moment of surrender. A memory came back to me, one from Susan's vault. Snow over London, the rookeries glistening white, a full moon in the icy sky. Jacob's Island, crooked and bent, but somehow resplendent in its new cloak of snow. Beautiful, but cold beyond reason. Susan, with three other girls, huddled in a doorway, watching the night; the Island eerily still.

Something reached my ears. Hard to catch against the raging wind, but something... a whistle. Somebody whistling a tune. Only snatches of its melody came through at first, but then I deciphered it. *Silent Night*. O Holy Night.

I opened my eyes and looked about me. White swirling walls. I looked to my hands. They were red raw. I could no longer feel them.

The whistling again. Closer now. Behind me.

I turn around, but then the whistling came from my left. It was circling me, closing in. Then a voice came along the wind, *"Come up here..."*

It was a man's voice. Deep, guttural.

"Come up..."

A higher pitch now.

"Come up, come up..."

I couldn't see a shape, but nevertheless backed away from the direction of the voice.

"Come up, come up and be..."

Closer still. I wasn't sure if I could make out a figure or not, or if the vortex was playing the trickster with my eyes.

"Come up..."

I turned to run.

"Come up..."

The black scrag was stood before me. His face like an ancient tree, black hair blowing about in the wild white, making him look like some Old Testament Prophet. His eyes were marble black. His form shifted uncannily in the storm.

He opened his mouth. It was black, and this blackness, this essence of him, ran from his mouth like hot tar. It stank. Putrid; a decaying thing.

"Come up," he said. *"Come up and be dead."*

He was Ranskul in life. In death, he was a black scrag, a token of misery.

"Come up and be dead."

His black dripping mouth opened wide, and wider still. The blackness drooling from his jaws in long tendrils. A maw wide enough to swallow me whole.

I screamed then. *We* screamed, the women within me. The many lives that had harboured this soul. I heard all the voices within me. I heard Judy, from the megalopolis, Susan, from the low place, and others too. A peasant, a witch – or at least, woman burned as a witch – a tribal woman, a woman of no language, a cave-dweller; a legion of women whose lives I had lived.

The black maw, oozing its unholy sulphur, awaited my surrender, but the women within me, their screams turned to a battle cry, a harmony of force and reckoning.

The scrag made a noise, an unearthly cry, and the maw closed. *We* stood our ground. The scrag's black eyes rolled white. It shifted back from us as we raged with all our strength. Make those black hills tremble.

The scrag's form shifted against the storm, elongating, and finally breaking apart and scattering on the wind. Its face stretched upward, torn asunder, enveloped by the white.

Then it was gone.

Our voices died, and I was left alone once more.

I fell to the snow.

I lay on my back, breathing hard. I heard a noise on the wind, an engine perhaps. I listened, and thought about all the lives I had led, and all the lives I will lead in the many ages to come. The endless circle.

The noise was closer now. It was definitely a vehicle. A snowcat perhaps, Ajáito at the wheel. I wondered if he'd find me out here, if he'd reach me in time. I could no longer feel my body, this transient flesh.

I heard the engine stop close by, then I heard my name being called, "Miss Judy, Miss Judy…"

"Here," I whispered, and fell into the vortex.

I've got a story for you. I suppose you could describe it as a ghost story, but not in any classical sense. It's not set in some gothic mansion haunted by pasty white kids in Victorian garb or hooded monks or any of that shit. It's something that happened to me twenty years ago, in the winter of 1999, when I was 19.

It happened in a normal terrace house on an everyday street round the back of my old school. A house on Lidderman Street.

That year I was working as a bricklayer's labourer. Anthony Valender was the brickie's name. He had a gang of blokes – a couple of old boys named Les and Harold, some rough-arse psychopath named Rob – and we'd all cram into the back of Valender's shitty white van and go off each day to this job and that.

I'd mix cement – gobbo, as the lads called it – and load them out with bricks and blocks and generally keep them going all day. Ant and Rob were fast as well, and it was pretty relentless work keeping them in gear. Les and Harold were a bit easier to manage.

In return for my valiant services, Ant and Rob took it upon themselves to provide me with what they described as 'some much-needed character building' and took the piss out of me from morning till night. This was very kind of them and in no way did I want to wrap my shovel round the back of their heads.

Rob was a particularly nasty piece of work, but Ant was only marginally better. After all, he was the one who locked me in a portaloo and tipped it over, and pushed me in some footings as we were pouring wet concrete. He'd find these antics highly amusing, and if I got angry or upset, he'd usually tell me to stop being such a cry-baby and take the piss even more. One time they nailed me to a concrete floor – nine-inch nails through my jeans and the sleeves of my shirt. They even pulled my jeans down at the crotch and nailed me there (which was particularly nerve-wracking as the hammer swung millimetres from my bollocks). They left me there nailed to the floor all day. At lunchtime, Rob pulled down his trackie bottoms and gently placed his balls on my forehead, then, at the urging of Ant, he smudged my nose with his arse crack. They almost hyperventilated with laughter.

All this for a hundred and twenty quid a week.

Still, I suppose they were right about one thing – it certainly made for good character building.

The day I went to work at the house on Lidderman Street, I thought I'd be having the day off. It was in the January of that year and it had snowed heavily overnight. It was still dark when the alarm went off and I looked out of my bedroom window and saw the dim, white world outside. My immediate thought was *there's no way we're going out in that* and I settled back down.

I'd just started drifting off again when me mum started banging on the bedroom door. "Peter! Peter!" she shouted. "Get up!"

"Anthony's here," she said. "They're waiting for you!"

I couldn't fucking believe it.

I threw on my dirty work clothes – there's nothing worse than putting on days-old stinking work clothes on a freezing cold morning, in the dark – raced downstairs, grabbed me pack-up – which mum had already made me – got me boots on, and me coat, and stumbled out into the snow. It crunched beneath me as I walked to the van, which was sat idling by the curb.

I opened the back of the van, expecting to jump in with Les and Harold, but found only the mixer and a bag of tools. Ant's bag. Rob wasn't in the passenger seat either. There was only Anthony. "You can sit up 'ere," he said.

I shut the back doors and walked round to the passenger side. Our street was dead, not a car or soul about. The only tyre tracks in the snow were Ant's. No sod was out in this, only us.

I got in and Ant pulled away.

He didn't say a word.

I looked out the window. The world lay in an eerie stillness. Most houses were in darkness, some had lights on, but curtains were still drawn. It was 7 a.m. and I was dreading the day ahead.

I licked my lips and said, "Where are we going?"

"To work, you stupid cunt."

"I know, I mean... surely we're not going to the site?"

"Is your alarm clock broken?"

"No... I just..."

"Just what?"

"Just thought... we wouldn't be going in today."

"Why did you think that?"

"Cause...' I motioned to the still world beyond the windscreen. "The weather..."

"It's only a bit of snow."

"Yeah... suppose."

I fell silent. I couldn't believe that this was my life.

We passed a car on the other side of the road, struggling to get up a hill. The back wheels were spinning all over the place. Ant didn't say a word.

I took a pen from the dash and pushed the point against my leg.

"Where are the others?" I said.

"You ask a lot of a fucking questions, you do."

"Just wondered."

I applied more pressure and dug the pen deeper into my leg.

"They're havin' one off," he said.

"Oh, right. But we're not?"

"No, *you're* not. You're in all this week, lad."

He didn't elaborate, and I didn't ask. I dropped the pen into the foot-well. I thought about telling him to pull over and getting out of the van right then and there, but I didn't. A tolerance for abuse is quite amazing when you're young.

We passed my old school, then turned left into Lidderman Street. I hadn't been on the street for years. I told myself that this job wasn't my life, and that this prick beside me didn't have anything on me. It didn't work.

We pulled up outside number 12. There were no curtains up, and the place was in complete darkness. It looked empty.

"Hope you're wearing your thermals," Ant said, and got out the van.

I followed Ant up the pathway to the front door. There were piles of snow-covered rubbish in the front garden. Chairs, a broken-up wardrobe, a bed-frame, and other odds and sods.

There was a pale light in the sky. Day was finally breaking. It was bitterly cold.

Ant searched for a particular key on his thick bunch and said, "You'll be here all week."

He found the key, shoved it into the lock, and opened the door.

I could smell the house immediately. It smelt fusty, damp, the smell of age and loneliness. We stepped inside. Somehow, it felt even colder.

Ant flicked on the light and a naked bulb flickered into life. A narrow hallway led to rooms off to the left, and to the stairs off-set to the right. The hallway was empty – no carpet, no wallpaper, no life. This was a house stripped back to the shell.

Ant moved down the hall and took the door on the left. I followed.

He again flicked on the light and illuminated the front room, complete with bay window, also empty. The floorboards looked rotten and there was mould around the windowsill. Every noise we made sounded hollow.

There was an opening in the wall opposite the bay window which led to a small backroom, followed by a narrow-length kitchen, and a downstairs toilet added on the back of the house. Ant walked through to the backroom and I followed him.

There were several large tubs of paint and a few rollers, along with brushes and a pack of fresh sandpaper. I realised my fate.

"I need the whole house doing," he said. "Both these rooms, the kitchen, toilet, hallway, then the three bedrooms upstairs, plus the toilet and landing. Walls and ceiling, and I've got you plenty of matt for the skirtings and door frames. Leave the doors because they're all being replaced."

"On my own?"

"Yes, on your own. I've got another job on. Wash your brushes out properly as well, I ain't buying anymore."

"Whose house is this?"

"Nobody's at the moment. Nobody that wants to live here anyway. It's to sell on so make a good job. Don't worry about getting paint on the floors, it's gonna be carpeted throughout, but that doesn't mean you can just throw it about. There's a stepladder upstairs for the ceilings and such. I'll pick you up at five."

He walked to the opening, then turned to look at me. "And don't fuck about,' he said. 'You've got till Friday to finish it, otherwise I'll be docking you."

With that, he was gone.

I listened as he walked down the hallway, opened the front door and slammed it shut behind him. I stood looking at the paint, then, as I hadn't had a chance yet that morning, I went and had a piss in the downstairs toilet. The bowl was filthy and stank. The sink was the same.

The narrow kitchen was falling to bits. The units, which hadn't been updated for several decades, were worn and crooked and rotten at their base. The fridge was ancient; I opened it and found nothing inside other than a terrible smell and something growing in one corner.

I decided to check upstairs before I got started, and walked back through the rooms to the hallway. I went up the stairs and found myself on a landing. I could see my breath pluming out before me.

There were two main bedrooms, a front and a back to the left, and the bathroom and a small box room to the right. I went in the box room first, which overlooked Lidderman Street. All was still quiet and semi-dark. I then checked the toilet (the bath was seriously grim), then the front bedroom, which was a fairly good size. It contained nothing but the small stepladder Anthony had mentioned.

In the back bedroom, I left the light off and walked across to the window. I got a view of the gardens along Lidderman Street. The house's garden was completely overgrown, and it looked to me like bulky, white shapes were trying to gain access. The other gardens along the row were neat and well-kept; sheds and greenhouses, lawns and fishponds, and kids climbing frames. There was a tree line beyond the gardens, through which I could glimpse the main road and the lower form block of my old school. The snow gave the world an extra dimension; a melancholic and haunting quality.

I went back downstairs.

Having missed breakfast, I ate one of the sandwiches from my pack-up, and watched the sky lighten over Lidderman Street. I was pretty cold, so figured I'd better make a start, if only to try and keep warm. All the paint was white, which simplified things, and I cracked open one of the tubs and poured a good deal into a tray. All the rollers and brushes were brand new.

I decided to start in the downstairs toilet and work through the house. The ceiling was lower in the toilet than the rest of the rooms, so I didn't need the stepladder. It looked to be an extension, added long after the house had originally been built. I took my tray and roller through the kitchen into the toilet and rested the tray on the sink. I needed some fresh air in there to combat the stink, so I opened a small window, figuring it was freezing anyway, so what difference would it make. There were a few cobwebs in top corners, so I went back through to the middle room and found a rag, then returned to the toilet to wipe them all away. That done, I set to work.

I painted pretty much flat out for the next hour or so. I got the ceiling done and three of the walls. It was a small room, so didn't take that much doing. After that, I took a breather. My arms ached, and I looked at my watch: 9:20. It felt like I'd already been there for hours. I dropped the roller in the tray and stepped out of the toilet.

I decided to open the backdoor in the kitchen and so rummaged about trying to find a key. I looked in several of the units, finally finding one single key in a drawer by the sink. I tried it, and with a bit of persuasion the door unlocked.

I stepped out into the snow. The day was bright now, the winter sun burning through the cloud cover. The snow glimmered.

The garden was certainly overgrown and looked to be pretty much impassable after a certain point. There were a couple of garden chairs, collapsing under the weight of their own age, and a steel bin. I wished I'd brought along a radio, something to keep me company on this impossibly long day. I was also hungry and only had one sandwich, a packet of crisps, and a banana left. In the rush that morning, I'd forgotten to pick up my flask, so I didn't even have anything to drink. I knew there was a corner shop not far from my school, but I didn't have any money on me, so that was out. There was nothing for it but to simply get on and try and get the job done as soon as possible.

I went back inside and shut the backdoor behind me. As I moved through the kitchen something made me stop. A feeling; my spine reacting.

I turned around and looked through the kitchen, through the middle room, and into the front room beyond. I could see the bay window and the white world outside. I stood and listened to the house. There was birdsong outside, and the sound of either a bus or lorry out on the main road. But the house... the house remained silent.

I shook it off and went back into the toilet and continued with the last wall. I probably should have got out of the house right then and there, but I suppose it's easy to say that in retrospect.

What I did was work solidly for the next hour or so. I finished the toilet – walls, ceiling, doorframe and skirting – and then moved on to the kitchen. I used the brush to get round the units. I figured the entire kitchen was going to be ripped out, so my painting the parts of the wall that could be seen was probably futile, but Anthony had said to do the whole house, so that's what I planned to do. As there were so many units, it didn't take me long. I didn't bother doing behind the fridge.

Those two rooms done, I moved straight into the middle. I needed the stepladder to reach the ceiling, so I went back upstairs. I went into the front bedroom, grabbed the ladder, then went back out into the landing. It was here I stopped.

My senses alerted me to something watching me from the back bedroom. I felt goose-bumps break out on my legs and arms. My spine quivered. It was dark out on the landing.

I stood, looking down the stairs, to the front door. I didn't dare turn around.

The hairs of my neck bristled and my imagination went into overdrive. I couldn't hear anything, but I certainly felt it. I imagined a hand reaching for me, sensed the tips of its fingers inches from my neck. I shivered, and the jolt that shot through my body got me going. I dropped the ladder and leaped down the stairs, taking several steps at once, not looking back. I raced through the front room and came to rest in the middle room, panting.

I'd left the backdoor open to air the kitchen and downstairs toilet, and sunlight streamed in. The sun, and the open door, reassured me. The door gave me an escape, the sun gave me light.

I looked at my watch: 11:11.

I somehow decided that I was safe down here, in the light, that the problem was upstairs. Then I tried to analyse exactly what that problem was, and I couldn't come up with an answer. Not an answer I wanted to accept anyway.

I laughed it off and figured I'd better just get back to work. Then I realised I still needed to get the stepladder. I groaned and had to sit down.

I leaned against the wall and listened to the house, listened hard.

Everything was still.

Then, very faintly, I heard a tapping. Rhythmic, 1,2,3,4, then stop, then pick up again. It was coming from directly above me, in the back bedroom. It sounded like a finger tapping on the bare floorboards.

I looked up at the ceiling and tried to locate its exact position. Tap, tap, tap, tap, 1,2,3,4, coming from the middle of the ceiling, just to the right of the naked light bulb.

Then, it stopped. I held my breath.

I heard the far away laughter of children playing out in the snow.

There was a movement to my left, in the kitchen.

I drew back, banging my head against the wall. The knock made me squeeze my eyes shut. I rubbed the back of my hair, then I opened my eyes.

There was a large black bird stood on the step that divided the kitchen and the middle room. It was looking at me with curious, beady little black eyes.

It was a raven, or a crow. I couldn't be sure, but it was tall, and black, and bold as brass.

There was a dusting of snow on its feathers, and around the point of his beak. Its black eyes looked at once lifeless and yet, all knowing.

It squawked at me. An awful sound in the hollow house.

I got up, waving my hands wildly. "Get out!" I cried.

The black bird squawked and hopped and flapped its wings. I came towards it fast, "Out! Out!"

It took off and flew straight out of the backdoor. I followed it out and watched it as it took to the sky. It disappeared from view. The clouds looked low and heavy now. More snow was on the way.

I went back into the house and marched straight through to the hallway and up the stairs. Once at the top of the landing I went to each and every door and kicked them open, throwing in as much light as I could.

"I'll tell you what," I said. "You leave me alone, and I'll leave you alone."

I left a pause for a reply that never came.

"Let me get me job done and I'll be out of your way. We clear?"

Nothing.

"Good."

I picked up the stepladder and went back downstairs.

I set the ladder up in the corner by the kitchen, then topped up the tray. Before I set to work, I shut the backdoor.

I painted over the cobweb in the corner and rolled white across the ceiling. I began to sing as I worked. In the back of my mind rattled a memory of being told that singing was a good way to ward off evil spirits, so I thought what the hell and sang Oasis' 'It's Gettin' Better (Man!!)' at the top of my voice.

I don't know if it would ward off any spirits, but it certainly lifted mine. That song, that band, made me think of nights out with me mates, summer nights with warmth and laughter and girls and drink and freedom.

I rolled, moved the steps, and rolled again. Singing as loud as I could. *It's gettin' better, man.* I drifted into a kind of a medley of songs off *Be Here Now*, and picked up the refrain from 'All Around the World.' *And I know what I know…*

I blocked out the house, the winter, the cold, and lost myself in the motion of my actions, and the songs, and memories that filled me; the faces and events of the things that shaped me. I went into myself.

I liked being there.

A loud thud knocked the past from me.

It came from the front room. I stood, breathing hard. Then there was another thud. Something was hitting the bay window. I dropped the roller in the tray and rushed into the next room.

Snowballs were sliding down the window.

"Fuckers," I said, and stormed down the hallway and out the front door.

Three boys were out in the road. When they saw me come running out of the empty house, they legged it.

"Oi!" I shouted. I could hear them laughing as they ran down the street.

My heart was thumping against my chest, but I smiled. I was one of those kids once, playing down Lidderman Street. This was a street of families, of kids that went to my old school. This was England at the end of the century, coming down from five years of seemingly endless summer, a last party before the new millennium. This was not an isle of ghosts. This was no longer a land of superstitions; the devils and midnight freits had been put firmly at the very back of the British psyche. My life was shitty work, living for the weekend, drinking, smoking gear, getting off with girls down town, and buying records. That was my life. That was clear and real to me. I wouldn't be spooked by a decrepit old house. Fuck that.

I walked back inside actually believing the shit I was telling myself.

I continued painting for another half an hour or so, then I had my pack-up. I wolfed down my remaining sandwich and the crisps and then the banana in no time. After that I was pretty thirsty and so I went and turned on the tap in the kitchen. Water spluttered out, pipes banging and clattering through the house. It looked murky at first, then ran itself clean, and I ducked my head under and took a drink.

When I straightened up and took a look into the middle room I saw that the tray was upturned and white paint was steadily running along the floor boards. I walked over and crouched down before it. I watched as the paint filled the joints and trickled towards the opening to the front room.

I looked at my watch. It read: 11:11.

I tapped the face, and shook my wrist, trying to shock it back into life. I felt disorientated and a little lightheaded. Then the tapping came again. 1,2,3,4, on the floor above me. The tap of a fingernail. Tap, tap, tap, tap, pause, tap, tap, tap, tap. Faint, but unmistakably there.

I righted the tray, then walked out of the middle room and into the front room. I saw it had started to snow again. Heavy flakes, silently falling. I went out into the hallway and ascended the stairs. I didn't rush, I didn't panic. I put one foot in front of the other and came to the landing. All the doors were closed again and the tapping continued from behind the backroom door.

I walked across the landing and gripped the door knob. The tapping was louder now. I turned the knob, but the door wouldn't budge. I looked down and saw a key poking out of the door. I turned it, heard the lock click, then tried the door again.

Tap, tap, tap, tap.

The door opened. I pushed it into the room, but I remained stood on the threshold. The tapping stopped, the room was empty.

I stepped inside. "Oh, of course there's nobody here," I said, loud enough for the whole house to hear. "Why would there be?"

I walked across to the window and watched the snow fall outside. I could no longer see my old school.

I heard a click behind me. My spine reacted to this, as did my skin. I knew without a doubt that there was someone in the room with me.

I turned around.

The door was closed. The room was empty. Empty to my eyes, at least.

I could hear my heart, but nothing else.

"Hello," I whispered.

Nothing.

Then the tapping came again. *Tap, tap, tap, tap*, 1,2,3,4, from the centre of the room, but I couldn't see anything. Then there came a scraping, like fingernails being dragged along the wood flooring.

There is a surreal element to being faced with the supernatural. It doesn't feel entirely real, even when it is happening in front of you, and this detachment gives you a thrill. You feel the fear, but your logical mind tries to counter the event with rational answers – rats in the floorboards, faulty piping, whatever – and this dichotomy of senses gives you a kind of momentary lapse of reason. Through the fear, and the crawling skin, you develop a sense of humour. It can't possibly be real, even though something fucked-up weird is happening right in front of you, so you take the piss. You laugh at the ridiculous unreality of it all.

"What the fuck is that?" I said. "Is that all you're gonna do, tap on the floorboards? Really fucking scary."

Even as I was saying this, I felt all my senses prickling wildly. My body reacted to a shift in the room. I thought my legs were going to give out, but somehow I remained standing. I felt the *presence* swoop towards me.

It faced me. I could feel it there, even though I couldn't see it. The humour, the ridiculous nature of it all, left me, deserted me, and all that remained was absolute terror.

I felt myself shaking. My mouth was open, and I felt drool run down my chin. I couldn't move.

Then its fingernails gently touched the side of my neck. I felt their sharpness, their jaggedness. I cried out and fell back against the wall, collapsing onto the floorboards.

I covered my face with my hands. I could sense the thing standing over me, looking down at me. Then... then there was nothing. It was gone.

I lowered my hands and opened my eyes. It was still snowing outside. The house was still.

I went to stand up when a sudden force pushed me back down. I screamed. Two large hands grabbed my left ankle and jerked me across the floor. I banged the back of my head against the floorboards. The thing dragged me to the centre of the room, then I felt a heavy weight on my chest. Those nails, those long fingernails, clawed at my skin, my neck, my face, and ripped at my clothes. I flailed my arms around, trying to fight it off, but I could not connect with the thing. It connected with me though.

My mind became paralysed, a swirl of blackness. The survival instinct kicked in and I struggled and fought. I tried to scramble away, but each time the thing would drag me back and slash at me, claw at me. I tasted blood in my mouth, could feel wounds leaking all over my body.

At one point I opened my eyes and looked up to the window and saw the snow still falling. A fingernail scratched close to my eyes and I squeezed them shut again.

The large hands gripped my neck and I choked, but then it must have decided that clawing at me was more fun, so it released its pressure on my throat and dragged its nails into my windpipe.

I raged, I screamed. "That's enough!"

It stopped. Its weight was still on my chest, but the frenzied attack ceased.

"That's enough," I said. "You've had your fun."

The thing got off me. I was allowed to sit upright and rest against the wall. The snow outside looked beautiful.

"No more..."

I sensed the thing stood over me. I realised I was crying.

There was a shift in the room, and then a click and the door opened.

I winced as I stood up. My entire body felt bruised, my head felt foggy.

I walked to the door and then paused. I glanced around the room, then looked to the snow outside. I could see my breath. I was alive.

"I've got painting to do," I said to the room.

I walked out and closed the door behind me.

I went back downstairs and stripped to the

waist. I shivered and washed my face and chest in freezing cold water. The cuts and scrapes were very painful. I examined them, prodding them, opening up the cuts, watching the blood seep out. I felt my erection.

I used my t-shirt to dry myself with, then threw it on the floor as I redressed in my shirt, jumper and coat. I shivered hard and returned to my work in an effort to get warm.

It did the trick. I furiously painted the middle room, practically throwing paint at the walls.

Above me there were bangings and scrapings and doors slamming open and shut, open and shut.

I carried painting in a kind of fever dream. My eyes locked in on the roller, back and forth, back and forth. I felt out of myself, completely detached. The cuts and scrapes, nicks and bruises throbbed. Paint would drip onto a wound and it would sting and I would smile.

I wondered who I was. I was confused by my nature. My proclivities.

Once the middle room was done, I headed back upstairs and stood outside the back bedroom. It was falling dark outside and I could see my breath.

I went back inside the room. This time it was me who shut the door. I crossed the room and waited by the window. The snow had slowed, fluttering down in whispers. I felt the thing at my neck. I closed my eyes and was knocked from my feet and dragged across the room.

This time the thing was even more brutal. It tore and slashed and bit at my flesh. Its teeth were sharp. If it got too severe and hurt too much, I would tell it to stop, otherwise it had free rein to do with me what it wanted.

I don't know how long it lasted, but when it was done with me it went away and I lay on the floor, panting, looking at the dark window and the flecks of snow steadily falling.

I lay there for a long while, feeling the blood leak from me from here and there. I wiped some with my hand and licked it off. I enjoyed the taste of iron.

After a time, I went back downstairs and continued on with my work, although my vision wasn't quite right. I moved into the front room, but things seemed a little blurry. Still, I pressed on. I did the ceiling in no time, and then started on the walls.

All was quiet upstairs.

I looked at my watch: 11:11.

I wondered what time it was and how long it would be before Ant arrived to pick me up. It crossed my mind that he wouldn't pick me up, that the snow had made the roads too treacherous, and that I'd have to walk home.

I continued to work. I had to take off my coat as I could feel the sweat running down my back. The tapping started up again upstairs. It was waiting for me.

After another hour I was pretty much done with the front room. Then lights arced across the room and I looked out and saw Anthony's white van pull up. I saw two figures in the van. They got out and walked up to the house. It was Ant and Rob. I could hear the crunching snow.

Ant saw me looking at him through the window. Something about me must have unnerved him because he gave me the strangest look.

I heard the key in the front door and realised the thing had stopped tapping.

I heard them walk down the hallway and then I saw Ant appear at the doorway. He looked at me. He looked confused about something. He said, "What the hell happened to you?"

"Nothing," I said, my voice flat. "I fell off the ladder and cut myself."

"You better not have fucked up my steps?"

"No, they're fine."

Rob appeared behind him. "Alright, wank splat. Someone given you a good hidin' or summat?"

Ant turned to him and said, "Twat said he fell off the ladders."

Rob laughed, then looked at me. "You alrete, young un?"

I nodded.

Ant looked around the room. He inspected the ceiling, and the walls, then poked his head in the next room, turning the light on in there to see.

"You've done alright, lad. Kitchen done as well?"

"Yes, and the toilet."

"Your cutting-in's a bit sloppy, but it'll do I suppose."

"I thought you'd 'ave bin pullin' your pud all day," said Rob. "But looks like you've been cracking on all right. Might make somethin' out of you yet."

I fingered a cut in the palm of my hand, driving my nail into the opening.

"What time is it?" I asked

"Seven," said Ant.

"I thought you were coming at five?"

"You seen it out there. You're lucky we came at all."

"Who owns this house?"

"Why do you want to know?"

"Just wondered."

Rob cut in. "You're acting fuckin' weird."

"Just tell me." I said.

"You what, you cheeky cunt?" said Ant. "I own it, alright? Nosy fucker."

"Good."

"What do you mean, good?"

"Just, good. I'm glad you own it."

Ant narrowed his eyes at me.

"Come on," he said. "Let's go before this weather gets any worse. They expect more snow tonight."

"I want to show you something first."

"You what?"

"Upstairs."

"What is?"

"Just come with me. Both of you."

"He's fuckin' barking orders out now," said Rob.

I walked past them and out into the hallway. I didn't wait for them to follow. I just started on up the stairs. They followed me, after a moment, bounding up the stairs after me.

I stood on the landing waiting for them.

"What is it?" said Rob. "A dead rat or somethin'?"

"Come," I said. "I'll show you."

I walked across the landing and pushed opened the door to the back bedroom.

"It's in there," I said.

Ant pushed past me and entered the room. "What is?" he said.

Rob followed him in.

Once they were in, the door slammed shut. I heard them both curse.

I turned the key, locking the door.

I saw the doorknob turn and rattle and the door strain as Ant and Rob tried to open it. They started banging on the door. "Stop fuckin' around, Pete. Let us out!"

"I'm gonna batter you to fuck."

"Open it!"

"Fuckin cunt!"

Fists slammed against the door, then they stopped. The house fell silent.

I heard a rush in the room and a loud thud. Then Anthony started screaming.

Rob started to bang on the door again, pleading to be let out, all the malice gone from his voice, but I didn't unlock the door. I listened, pushing my nail deeper into the cut.

Finally, I went downstairs. I washed all the brushes, rollers and tray, put the lid back on the paint, then I put my coat on.

The noise above me was very loud. Anthony was still screaming, as was Rob. I heard bodies being dragged and thrown about, and then I heard Ant's screams turn to pleas for help, for it to stop. He screamed for me, and for God, but neither one of us came to his rescue. I heard Rob whimpering like a little boy. It was quite sweet.

I stepped out of the house and nestled my chin into my coat. Before I shut the door I heard one final scream, this one horrific; the scream of someone in agony; the scream of someone realising that the horror was not going to stop.

I shut the door, shutting off the sound of the horrors going on inside number 12. I walked to the road, past Anthony's white van, and walked down Lidderman Street in the direction of home.

I never saw Rob again after that. I heard he moved away, but what became of him I do not know. I did see Ant every now and again though. He became a drinker, an all-day and all-night drinker, and he pretty much lost everything. Last time I saw him he was walking with a cane and was shaking uncontrollably. His face was red and blotchy and his hair was white. He looked ancient, but was probably only about fifty. I believe he died a few years back.

As for the house on Lidderman Street, I broke in a few times after that and spent a little time in the back bedroom, but once it was sold on, it was more difficult to break in. I stopped altogether eventually and tried to get help.

The house went from one owner to the next over the years, but they never stayed long. It was always up for sale.

Eventually it was taken off the market, permanently. It became so dilapidated that it was condemned and boarded up. It was demolished in 2012. It was a waste ground for a few years, but then someone bought the plot and they've built a new house on the site. A bland, lifeless, modern build. I've been by there once or twice.

I think about breaking in.

Two weeks before they visited their old school, Daniel Swathe tried to commit suicide. He fed a pipe from the exhaust of his car, into his side window, and sat on the front drive with the car ticking over. He'd seen it done this way in a film, and it'd seemed like a peaceful way to go.

It was night, and all the houses were dark. He felt numb, neither lamenting his life, nor regretting it. It was just something that had happened, and now, in his forty-fifth year, after years of trying and failing to understand the hollowness in his heart, it had to end. His life had run its course.

His wife Carol pulled him from the car just as the noise in his head was beginning to fade. She brought him back and held him and kept asking him *why*, again and again and again. She held him like a little boy, right there on the front drive. She cried like he'd never seen her cry before – a true, deep, haunted pain that he knew would never leave her. He realised then that this woman – who he'd known since they were was thirteen, who had been his wife for a quarter of a century, who he shared his life with – had no clue as to how he really felt, or who he really was.

He'd never talked to her, not properly, not deeply. He'd never told her that everyday felt like he was clinging on for dear life, that simply getting up, getting dressed, and going through the motions of life and work exhausted him beyond all reckoning. That the tiredness, and the hollowness, and the quiet desperation, permeated across every aspect of his life. He never told her any of this. He told no one.

Daniel Swathe, who read Paul Auster, and listened to Max Richter and Bob Dylan, and cried at the end of films, and loved his son, and played guitar, and smoked cigars in his shed, and enjoyed being with friends and laughing and remembering their collective pasts. This man.

Daniel Swathe, who had grown heavier in middle age, whose belly was now soft and whose beard was grey, and whose handshake was firm, and whose eyes were kind. This man was really only half a person. And nobody, not even his wife, could see it.

So, on the night Carol Swathe had found her husband trying to kill himself, something unlatched within her, something that could not be set right again. The life she had thought she was living, for all those years, was a lie. The man she thought she knew was a stranger to her.

Carol Swathe, who long ago had been Carol Broadly, all braces and acne and pleated skirts, who had first kissed Daniel Swathe round the back of the sports hall on a long ago autumn afternoon, realised that the boy she had known then, full of promise and optimism and laughter, had grown up alongside her, but not with her. He had grown into somebody else. Somebody very different from the man he presented to her, and to everybody else in their lives. He was somebody swallowed by darkness.

Daniel said he would see a therapist and he went back to work, and he and Carol talked a little, but neither of them knew what to say. They had surface conversations. Carol was angry at first, angry at him for being so willing to leave her with such wreckage. They talked about how many men take their own lives, particularly in middle age, and how social constructs deter men from talking about their feelings. Daniel said he hated the word *feelings*. He said it made him sound like he was some kind of morose teenager.

He cried a little, and Carol cried, and there was tenderness between them – how could there not be after thirty-two years of knowing one another – and then life carried on. But there was a scar; it was deep, invisible, but very much there, and they both knew it. It had been there a long time.

Carol found out about their old school being torn down from the local paper. It was set for demolition in the New Year, and in early December there was to be an open evening for ex-pupils of the school to take one last look around before it was gone forever.

Carol rang their mutual school friend, Lee, before she told Daniel about it. Carol and Lee spoke often and were very close still. Lee had married and divorced in his 20s, and then never bothered settling down again. Women came and went in his life, one after another, and there had been a chance, when he and Carol were in their early 30s, when an affair might have begun, but they both buried it, and buried it deep. They both loved Daniel too much to act on any impulses they may have had.

But that was a long time ago.

Lee was very into the idea of visiting their old school, and they both thought that it might be good for Daniel. It might remind him of who he was and where he'd come from. Nostalgia, they agreed, was good for the soul.

They'd looked up to Daniel in school; he was a force of nature back then, and to remind him of this, in the very place of so many beginnings, might have a kind of healing effect. Plus, Carol said, they really needed to get out of the house.

So it was set. Daniel reluctantly agreed at first, but as the day approached he began to get more excited by the prospect of visiting their old school. They began to reminisce more; their talk turned to the past, to their youth, and they both enjoyed this. They even began to have sex again; free, unselfconscious, youthful sex. He didn't hide his belly from her.

It snowed on the day of the opening. Carol watched it from her kitchen window as she waited for Daniel to return home from work. The snow fell gently, silently. The branches of the trees turned white by degrees. Carol had always felt the magic of snow. From girlhood she had retained the wonder in its ephemeral beauty. She saw herself and Daniel in that garden, their younger selves, playing with their son in the snow. She found that she was crying and was surprised at how painful the memory now felt.

Daniel arrived home at five. He was smiling when he walked in. He found his wife in the kitchen. All the lights were off and she was crying, watching the snow. He held her and told her that everything was going to be alright. They ate a light meal. They didn't talk.

They left around six thirty. Daniel drove. The roads were treacherous.

They picked Lee up before heading onto the school. It was good to have him in the car. He lightened the mood and they talked about the past.

They drove through familiar streets in a part of the town they rarely ventured anymore. The streets of their youth. Their old stomping ground, as Lee referred to it.

They saw the school as they approached. All the lights in the buildings were on and it looked like a beacon, a lighthouse of memories.

It was a run-of-the-mill inner city comprehensive, built in the 1960s. They drove into the school grounds, the playing field white, the bike shed empty, the sports hall in darkness. There were two main blocks, a lower and an upper school. They pulled up in the staff car park by the upper school. Daniel turned off the engine.

"There aren't many other cars about," said Carol.

"Be the weather," said Lee.

They sat for awhile, nobody moving, then Carol said, "Haven't been here in so long."

Daniel looked at her. "Several lifetimes ago," he said, and opened his door.

They trudged through the snow to the upper school's main doors. They could make out a few figures moving about in the reception. The snow was deep and crunched under foot. They could see their breath. Daniel thought about the boy he once was.

They entered their old school.

Mrs Wood, their old headmistress, was there to greet them. Warm handshakes, pleasant smiles, electric charge of memories. She remembered them, especially Daniel. The teacher now looked ancient.

The place smelt the same: disaffection, old wood, adolescence. The assembly hall lay beyond the reception. All the lights were up bright. It was an insipid, lonely illumination. The assembly hall doubled as the school cafeteria back in the day, and probably still did. Daniel remembered that he ate fish fingers and chips pretty much every day for five years.

"So, what do you do now, Daniel?" asked Mrs Wood, reminding him that he was now a grown man.

"I work in an office."

"I thought you'd be a writer, or an artist of some kind," she said.

"No, no... that didn't work out." He felt Carol's hand grasp his.

"You were so full of ideas when you were here," continued Mrs Wood, oblivious to the brick in his heart. "All those plays, and stories, and I remember that film you made. What was it called?"

"*A Second Chance.*"

"Oh yes, very amusing it was. Didn't you rope Mr Green into being in it?"

"We did, yes. Is he still here?"

Her expression changed. "He retired five years ago, and I'm afraid he died last winter."

All three of them fell silent.

"It was a blow, yes, but we celebrated his life here, and we keep him in our hearts."

There were a few other ex-pupils milling about, but none Daniel recognised. Many were heading down a darkened corridor that he knew led to the stairwell, and to each classroom. He pictured the top floor.

"Now," said Mrs Wood. "You have the run of the place. We expected more of a turn out, but I suppose this snow put people off coming out. Still, you're here, along with a few others, and every classroom is open and all the lights are on. I'm sure you still remember where most things are. Nothing much has changed in the thirty years since you were last here. We've had a few renovations and the odd lick of paint in that time, but all the classrooms are where you left them. I'll stay down here in case any more visitors turn up."

"You here on your own, Mrs Wood?" asked Carol.

"Please, call me Mary, I don't think we need to be so formal anymore."

"I never knew that was your name."

"Yes, well... Larry Taylor was going to come, but he had car trouble, I expect because of the weather, and Eleanor Williams couldn't get through the snow either, so it is just me I'm afraid."

"I remember Mr Taylor," said Lee, "but not Eleanor Williams."

"She teaches Maths now Mr Borg has retired, so she's after your time. Anyway, please enjoy the school. I'll be sad to see it go."

"How long have you worked here?" asked Carol.

"Fifty-five years. I think it'll feel like a part of me is torn away when this place comes down."

They went into the Assembly hall first. Their voices echoed. Daniel went over to the great windows, put his hands around his face and peered out into the school yard. The technology block lay in darkness across the expanse of concrete. It all looked smaller than he remembered.

He then went over to the stage. He ran his hand over the wood flooring. Buffed and polished ready for demolition. He recalled seeing a touring production of Pinter's *The Dumb Waiter* on these boards. He recalled countless assemblies and Christmas plays and his own performances. He recalled kissing Carol in the wings, their faces so young.

Lee stood behind him.

"Remember that play we were in?" he said.

Daniel turned around. "Yeah, *The Little Drummer Boy.*"

"Ha, yeah, Jesus."

"You two were adorable in it," said Carol.

"John Chambers didn't think so," said Daniel, recalling the beating he'd received after the performance.

They all fell silent.

They moved down the darkened corridor. There was the Headmaster's office to the left, two ground floor classrooms which Daniel was pretty sure he never set foot in while at the school, then to the right, through double doors, the stairwell.

"This is so weird," said Lee.

"Yeah," said Carol. "It's like a dream."

They took the stairs. One flight to the first floor. There were four classrooms here, the first being Daniel's old form room. He recalled lining up outside this classroom, standing behind Carol, very close, smelling her hair. He looked at her now. There was grey at her temples, and crow's feet at her eyes, but she was still beautiful. She was the only woman he'd ever loved, the only woman he'd ever slept with, the only woman he'd truly ever known.

She smiled at him as they approached their old form room. He opened its door – the very same door – for the first time in twenty-nine years and allowed his wife and Lee to enter before he did.

He saw movement out on the stairway – the faintest glimpse of a shape, a figure – but when he looked there was nothing there. He thought, *it's happening again*, then went inside his old classroom.

"You two both sat over there," said Lee. "By the window."

"I liked looking at the playing fields," said Daniel.

"You were behind me," said Carol, "and I remember feeling you staring at me."

"Stalker," said Lee.

Daniel moved through the room.

"It seems so small," said Carol.

"Well, we're bigger now," said Lee.

"Speak for yourself." Carol went and sat at her old desk. "I'm pretty sure it was this one."

"It was," said Lee. "Danny, you go sit behind her."

He did.

Lee took a desk across the other side of the room, at the back, close to where he used to sit. The three of them sat, looking at one another, smiling, laughing, feeling incredibly strange.

Daniel spoke. "All the things we've done, since we were last here, in these places..."

"I know," said Carol. She turned around to look at him. Her eyes were watery.

Lee cut in. "You remember how long it took you to ask her out, Dan?"

Daniel looked at him. "No,' he frowned. "Not really."

"Fuckin' ages, mate. You kept talking about how much you liked her, but never actually did anything about it."

"I don't remember that."

"It was weeks. But I suppose weeks can feel like months when you're a kid."

"I didn't realise there was such a big build up," said Carol. "I feel quite honoured."

"We all skived off and went down the park," said Lee. "You remember?"

"Yes," said Carol. "Asked out by the swings, such romance."

"And if I hadn't have asked you out that day," said Daniel. "We wouldn't be here, having done all we've done. I might have asked you at some other point, but that would have led us down a different path. Lee shoving me in the back, telling me to do it, gave us the life we've lived."

"Why would it have been different if you'd asked me on a different day?"

"Because that would have led to a different set of circumstances. You might not have fell for me like you did if I'd waited."

"Who says I've fallen for you?"

Lee laughed.

"You know what I mean," said Daniel. "That day led to this day, and all the days in between."

"That was a good day then," she said, but her expression was strained.

On the second floor, they split up. Lee and Carol went into their old history class, and Daniel went into the room where he had taken geography with Mr Potts. There was a large world map on the back wall, very faded now. It was the same map his young self used to stare at every time he took the class.

The other walls were decorated with pictures from across the globe – the ridgeline of the Alps, a Caribbean Island, a Californian redwood forest, and many others, all new to him. But the world map was the same and he went and looked at it. All the places he thought he'd see and hadn't. The furthest he'd ever travelled was Spain.

His urge to travel was strong in youth, but now had diminished to almost nothing. Now he was happy to stay at home, with the TV on and lights up bright, which always made him think of that Joni Mitchell song. He knew he'd become that person, and he didn't care.

He found he was weeping.

He heard Lee and Carol talking in the classroom opposite. He went to the door and listened.

"How's he been?"

"Fine. It's like nothing ever happened. He's so... up."

"Really?"

"Yeah. He's almost manic and it's scaring me. I don't know what to say to him, how to be around him. I feel like if I say or do the wrong thing he'll go back to how he was."

"How bad was it?"

There was a pause. Daniel waited.

"He wouldn't talk to me. He wouldn't talk to anyone. He could barely look at me."

"And now he's hyper?"

"I think the suicide attempt gave him a jolt, and I know he feels bad and he's trying, but he's so all over the place at the minute... I'm just scared about where he's going to land, because he can't carry on like this."

Lee lowered his voice. "Do you ever talk about Christopher?"

"No. Not really. We both think about him all the time, but saying it out loud just... it's just too painful."

"It'll heal in time."

"It won't. It won't ever heal, Lee."

Daniel wiped his eyes and looked out to the stairwell. There were pockets of darkness on the stairs and Daniel sensed someone standing out there, watching him. He doubted it was an ex-pupil, and certainly wasn't Mrs Wood. He knew who it was and he couldn't bring himself to look any longer.

"Carol," he cried out.

Something in his tone panicked her and she came rushing out of the opposite classroom.

"What... what is it?"

Lee was right behind her. "You alright, buddy?"

"I'm fine," he said. "I just... I just want to go up to the top floor."

"Okay," said Carol, frowning. "Is that it?"

"Yes."

"But you sounded..."

"What?"

"You sounded frightened. Like really frightened."

He looked at them. Two people with whom he'd shared every aspect of his life with since he was thirteen. They both looked stricken with concern for him and it was painful, and yet, somehow humorous to watch.

He said, "Let's go to the top floor."

They stood in their old Maths class. Daniel had turned off the lights and they all stood at the window, looking out to the nearby houses, the odd chimney stack chugging out smoke. Most houses had lights on. They looked warm and inviting, nestled in the snow.

Over the rooftops, far off, twinkled the lights of the city centre. There didn't seem to be a soul about. The world was still, the school was still. Daniel shivered at the neck.

He closed his eyes and swallowed hard. It was time.

He said, "I've seen Christopher."

He felt his wife turn and look at him. He opened his eyes, but remained fixed on the night.

"What did you say?" said Carol. Her voice was very low, almost a whisper.

"I said, I have seen Christopher. More than once."

"What the fuck are you talking about?" Her voice was still low, laced with venom.

"His ghost. I've seen it."

Carol didn't anything for a long time. Daniel glanced at her. Lee was stood behind Carol, trying to read the situation. Carol, on the other hand, looked white, her eyes wide, anger radiating off her.

"Why would you say that?"

"Because I've seen him."

Now she raised her voice, and it was shocking in the darkness, in the quiet. "Don't you fucking dare bring Christopher into whatever your fucked-up mind is playing at now."

"Carol... please."

"Just shut up. Shut up."

Her voice cracked. Her pitch unnatural. Her words echoed around the dark classroom. Daniel looked to the night sky. Heavy clouds parted a little, and he glimpsed a sliver of moon.

"Please,' he said. 'You have to believe me. I've seen him... so many times."

Carol was crying now. She brought both hands up to her ears. Daniel raised his voice.

"Carol, listen. At first I thought I was dreaming, but it was him. Glimpses, shadows, his shape in my peripheral vision. Then once I saw him in our back garden. Near where his swing used to be."

"Daniel, I think you should stop this."

Daniel ignored Lee. "Then I started seeing him more and more."

Carol was now shuddering with sobs.

"Daniel!' shouted Lee. "Stop it!"

"Then I saw him the night I tried to..."

"DAN!"

"... tried to kill myself. I wanted to do it to be with him."

Carol smacked him in the mouth. Hard. Cutting his lip. It stunned him and he rocked back. All became quiet again.

There was only their breathing and the sound of someone moving about in the hall outside.

Daniel rushed out into the hall shouting his son's name. Carol and Lee went running after him.

There was no one out there.

"Daniel, stop this," screamed Carol. "For god sake, stop this."

"Carol, it's really him, please believe me."

Something in his voice, in his face, in his conviction, caused Carol's expression to change from one of fury, to one of pity, to complete and utter sorrow.

"Why would he be here?" she asked. "This is our place, not his. He never set foot in this school."

"He's following me."

"Oh come on, Daniel. How can you expect me to believe any of this?"

"Because I am your husband and your closest friend, and I've never lied to you. And you know I've never lied to you."

This shook her.

He continued. "I think he's lonely, and he wants us."

"Dan, stop," said Lee. "You're scaring her."

"Fuck off, Lee. This doesn't concern you."

"Don't speak to him like that," said Carol. "What do you mean he wants us?"

"Exactly that. He wants us to be with him. That's why... I was going to..."

"So you were going to leave me alone so you could be with our son?"

"Yes, but I wasn't in my right mind either."

"You're fuckin' tellin' me."

"But now I know, Carol. Now I truly understand. And I know you think I'm crazy, but our boy needs us. He's so lonely. We need to be with him."

"What the fuck are you saying? We both kill ourselves."

"Yes."

They fell silent.

Then Daniel said, "Nothing has ever felt right. I know that's hard for you to hear, but it's true. I've always had thoughts of killing myself, even when I young. This world is just too hard for me; this life is much too painful. When Christopher died, I knew there was no future for me. But seeing him... you don't understand... there's such melancholy in seeing a ghost. It's like that white world out there, beautiful, but tinged with such sadness. Winter is a season of decay; it's the end of things. The passing of life. Christopher is lost, wandering out in the snow, and we need to help him. We need to be with him."

"Do you know how insane you sound, Daniel?"

"As a matter of fact, I do."

"I carried him in my belly. He is part of me. I gave birth to him. He fed from my breasts and slept in my arms. I raised him. *We* raised him. He was a good boy, and could have been a strong and handsome and loving man. But he died, Daniel. We need to accept that and move on. You have to let him go... for your sake. For our sake. Please, Dan..."

She stopped then. She was overwhelmed.

The tears were blinding. Her legs felt weak and she stumbled. Lee caught her and held onto her.

Daniel just stood and looked at his wife, the mother of his dead son, and knew there was now no way back.

There came footsteps running down the stairs. They all heard it, and Carol was shocked to silence.

Daniel was the first down the stairs, Carol close at his heels. Lee followed. They could still hear someone rushing down the stairwell, and even though Carol kept looking over the banister, down and down to the darkness below, she glimpsed not a soul.

Daniel was ahead of her, but only a little way. He was breathing hard. She thought she heard him say Chris's name through ragged breaths, but she couldn't be sure.

The conviction with which he believed he was being haunted by their son's ghost was unnerving. Extremely unnerving. She could see that he really did believe it, and that had scared her more than anything. Worst of all, she found herself wanting to believe him.

An atheist since girlhood, she was rattled by her husband. He was right in that he had never lied to her, not to her knowledge, and had always been straight as an arrow with everyone they knew. He detested liars, in point of fact. He'd once gotten very angry with Christopher when he'd pulled the usual teenage ruse of saying he was staying at his friend's, when really he was out all night drinking down the park. Carol suspected there were girls involved in this all-nighter, and was mildly amused (herself, Daniel, Lee and others had done the very same in their youth, after all), but Daniel had been furious and came down hard on Chris. He hadn't been angry about him drinking all night down the park, he was angry that Christopher had felt the need to lie to them.

It was inconceivable that he'd knowingly lie about such a thing as seeing their dead son's ghost. He truly believed that he was seeing Christopher, and Carol really didn't know what to do with that. She was completely unable to process it.

She felt herself bounding down the stairs in a kind of daze. She felt detached from everything going on. And what was going on? Were they chasing their dead son's ghost down their old school stairs? She stifled a laugh.

The footsteps below them fell away and Daniel stopped, breathing hard.

"Who was that?" Carol asked, knowing full well what Daniel's answer would be.

"Our son. He's scared, Carol. He needs us."

"Stop this, Daniel. I don't believe in ghosts. You know that. *You* don't believe in ghosts."

"That was before…"

"I know you want this to be true, but it isn't. Our son is not haunting you. This is our old school, remember? The place where we began. You've been through a lot of emotional strain. We both have…"

There was a noise behind them and Lee appeared. He looked deathly pale.

Carol looked at him, blinking back tears, then said, "What's wrong?"

"I watched you. Both of you, from the top of the stairs. I stared straight down and…"

"And what?"

"And… I caught a glimpse of someone two flights below you. A boy."

Carol caught her breath. "What are you saying, Lee?"

"I'm saying I saw Christopher. He was near the bottom of the stairwell… it was just a glimpse, but it was him, Carol…"

She backed up against the wall. The tears fell.

She looked from Lee to Daniel, then to Lee again. These two men in her life. Two men she trusted above all others.

Her expression darkened. She wiped her eyes and said, "You fuckers."

"What?" said Lee.

Daniel said nothing.

"You pair of cunts. How dare you do this to me."

"Carol…"

"Shut the fuck up, Lee. This is a sick joke. You absolute fucking cunts."

She pushed past Daniel and descended the stairs at speed.

Daniel watched her go.

Lee ran past him, calling his wife's name.

Daniel ran his hand over the banister and recalled sliding down them when he was a boy. A boy not much older than Christopher. He went over to the window and looked out. Fog was rolling in. The snow sparkled. He could see his breath. It looked like the fog.

He knew with certainty that this would be his last night on earth.

Carol came running down the hallway, crying, raging, almost stumbling to the floor. Mrs Wood rushed to her. She was a frail woman and could hardly steady Carol, but she tried.

"Dear Lord, what happened?"

"They... they played a trick on me."

"Who did?"

Carol turned and pointed to Lee, who was running down the hall to meet them.

"Carol,' he called. "Carol, it's not a trick."

"Fuck you, Lee."

"Carol, please," said Mrs Wood, clearly very frightened now.

"They said my son was here."

"What? Your son?"

"He died."

"Oh God, that's awful, I'm so sorry."

"Carol..." Lee came up alongside them.

"And they said..." Carol was in pieces. "They said he was here tonight."

Mrs Wood looked at Lee, her eyes like saucers, her mouth open.

"Why would you say that to her?"

Daniel came walking down the hall. Carol watched him from the cradle of Mrs Wood's arms.

"Tear this place down," he said, his voice echoing around the dead school. "Tear it down and take the memories and life and energy of youth and turn it all to dust. I no longer have a past. I no longer have a future. There is just this moment now, and the little time I have left."

"What are you saying?" said Mrs Wood.

Lee answered for him. "He's saying he's going to kill himself."

Mrs Wood looked positively stricken now.

Carol shook herself from the old teacher's embrace and walked up to her husband. She hit him, hard. In the face, the chest, the head. She punched him and he stood there and took it. Lee finally intervened and grabbed Carol's arms and dragged her back.

Daniel was bleeding from his mouth again, and his eyebrow. Blood ran down his face. He didn't move.

Lee pulled Carol to the school doors. Mrs Wood watched all of this in absolute horror.

Daniel finally allowed himself to wipe away the blood with the back of his hand. He looked at the streak of red on his skin.

Carol was screaming and pulling against Lee, but he got her out of the school and into the night.

Mrs Wood then looked at Daniel.

He smiled at her, although there was no warmth in it. He said, "Thank you for the trip down memory lane. That is all done with now."

He walked out of the school and didn't look back.

The fog was thick. Pockets of runny yellow marked where the street lights stood, but for the most part the world was enclosed. The snow had frozen over and was hard underfoot. The fog was icy cold and incredibly dense.

Daniel couldn't see Carol, but he could hear her. Her cries were deadened against the fogbanks. He walked in the direction of her voice. He could also hear Lee trying to calm her down, but she screamed back at him, using words that Daniel had hardly ever heard his wife use.

Their shapes emerged into being as he approached them. Then he could see them. Lee still had his hands fast around Carol's arms and she was pulling and kicking and screaming and raging against him.

"Carol," said Daniel. She stopped and looked at her husband as he appeared from the fog. Her eyes were wild.

"Carol... I love you. I love Christopher. I want to be with him. I want you to be with him too."

She blinked as if trying to focus. They were completely enclosed in the fog. It moved about them in silent tatters.

The smudge of lights from the school building suddenly went out and everything was quiet. So quiet. Then:

"*Mummy.*"

Carol gasped. Lee let her go and she fell to the snow.

She looked all around her, trying to find the direction of the voice.

"*Mummy.*"

Closer now.

To the right of her, the fog rolled along as if being pulled, and there, dressed in the suit he was buried in, was her son. Her beautiful boy.

She stood and stared at him. They all stared at him.

"*I'm so lonely,*" her boy said. She wasn't sure if she saw his mouth move, but she certainly heard the words in her head.

Then the fog moved and shifted in its preternatural way and Christopher faded from view.

Carol turned and looked at her husband. He was crying.

She stood. She placed one hand on her belly, then looked back to the place where her boy had been stood. There was now nothing but a wall of fog.

She then stepped towards her husband. She took his hand in hers and put her face to his. She touched his mouth and his tears and his humanity and then whispered in his ear.

The word she said was, "Together."

Lee began to cry.

Also by Andrew David Barker:

The Electric (Boo Books, 2013)
Dead Leaves (Black Shuck Books, 2018)

*Now available and forthcoming from
Black Shuck Shadows:*

Shadows 1 – The Spirits of Christmas

by Paul Kane

Shadows 2 – Tales of New Mexico

by Joseph D'Lacey

Shadows 3 – Unquiet Waters

by Thana Niveau

Shadows 4 – The Life Cycle

by Paul Kane

Shadows 5 – The Death of Boys

by Gary Fry

Shadows 6 – Broken on the Inside

by Phil Sloman

Shadows 7 – The Martledge Variations

by Simon Kurt Unsworth

Shadows 8 – Singing Back the Dark

by Simon Bestwick

Shadows 9 – Winter Freits

by Andrew David Barker

Shadows 10 – The Dead

by Paul Kane

Shadows 11 – The Forest of Dead Children

by Andrew Hook

Shadows 12 – At Home in the Shadows

by Gary McMahon

blackshuckbooks.co.uk/shadows